John Kelly

A BEASTLY PIRATES ADVENTURE

MUNCH, CRUNCH, PIRATE LUNCH!

BLOOMSBURY
LONDON OXFORD NEW YORK NEW DELHI SYDNEY

The pirate leader, **Heartless Bart**,
had just received **bad** news:
The Beastly Pirates had
consumed **another** of his crews.

"What's wrong with all these COWARDLY swabs!" the pirate leader said. And **jammed** his giant tankard tight upon Tom Terror's **head**.

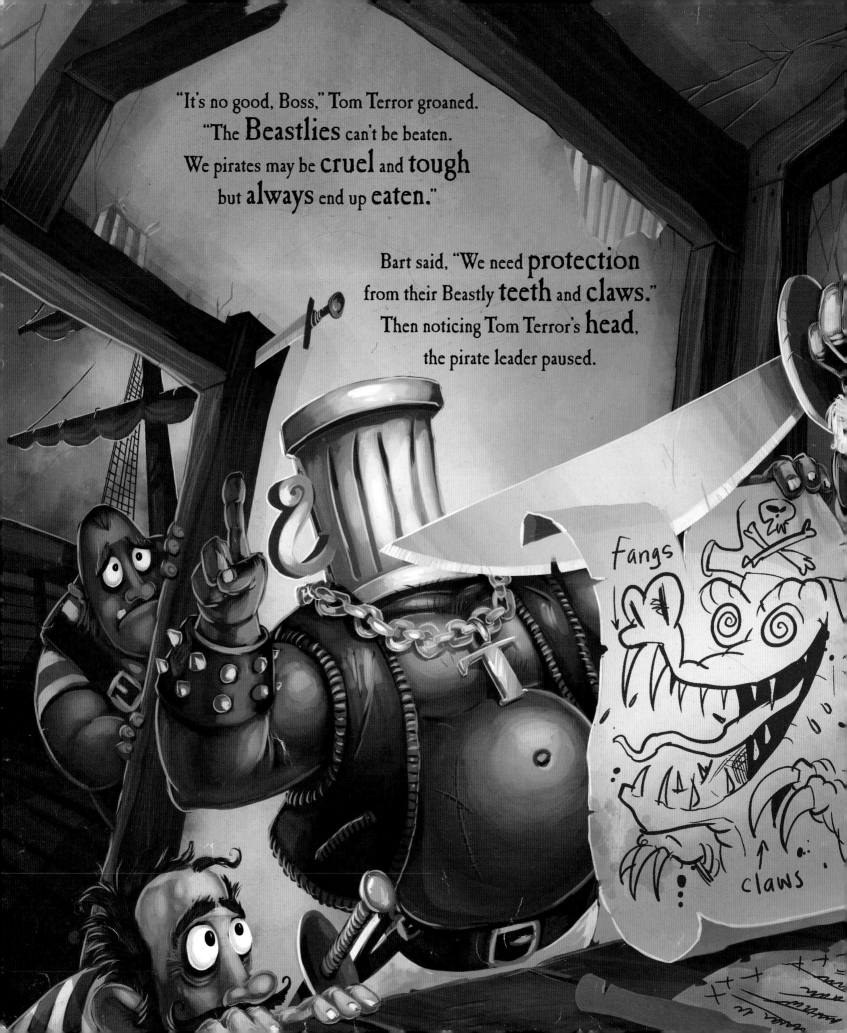

"It's no good, Boss," Tom Terror groaned.
"The **Beastlies** can't be beaten.
We pirates may be **cruel** and **tough**
but **always** end up **eaten**."

Bart said, "We need **protection**
from their Beastly **teeth** and **claws**."
Then noticing Tom Terror's **head**,
the pirate leader paused.

Fangs

claws

"Fetch the blacksmith, right away –
I've had an evil plan!
And round up every sword and axe
and knife and fork and pan."

Five days later, down the coast
and further out to sea,
the good ship **Beastly Pirate**
prowled the ocean **hungrily.**

Vic the Vulture squawked,
**"A Jolly Roger!
Dead ahead!**
It's time for **dinner**, Beastlies.
**GET THE OVEN
ON!"** he said.

The Beastlies **caught** the pirate ship
but **were** surprised to see
a **giant figure** on the deck,
who **gestured ANGRILY!**

He leapt **aboard** the Beastlies' ship;
there was **no** hesitating.
For Bart was clad
from **head** to **foot**
in **shiny**
armour
plating!

His right hand held a cutlass.
The left a gleaming **hook.**
And painted on his **metal face**
was a **cruel** and **wicked** look.

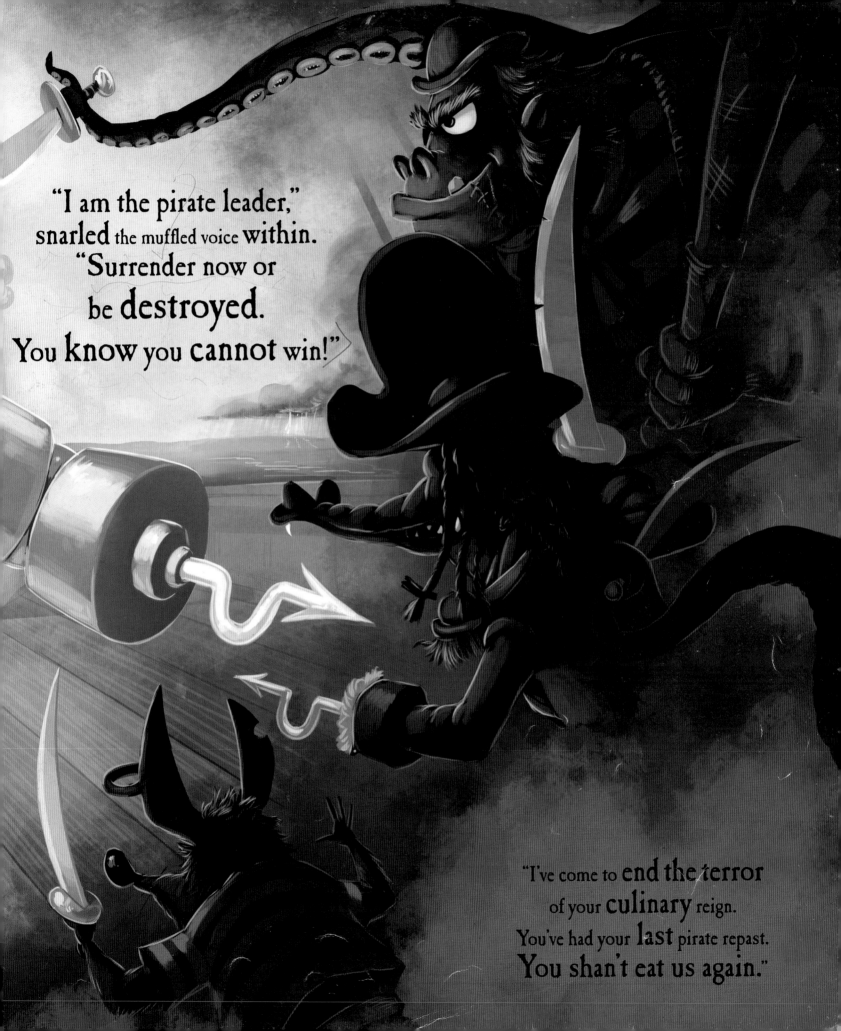

"I am the pirate leader," snarled the muffled voice within. "Surrender now or be **destroyed.** You **know** you **cannot win!"**

"I've come to **end the terror** of your **culinary** reign. You've had your **last** pirate repast. **You shan't eat us again."**

Razor Rhino
lowered his **horn**
and rushed Bart
really fast.

But *bounced* right
off his **armour**

and **embedded**
in the mast.

The *snarling*
Scurvy dog
dived in

and **bit Bart** on the **bottom.**

The metal **cracked** his front **teeth** and he lisped, **"That'th weally wotten."**

Bo'sun Beastly lashed ten oars together with a rope.
But when he **whacked** Bart's metal bonce, the wooden bundle **broke!**

"You can't hurt me!" sneered Heartless Bart, who sounded far too pleased.
And **bent** the Beastlies' weapons into **shapes** across his knees.

Krusher stuck his sticky suckers
onto Bart's cold steel.
But though he squashed and squeezed
and strained he couldn't make
Bart squeal.

The Beastlies heaved together
and aimed the ship's main gun.
Then Bo'sun Beastly lit the fuse
and counted...

3...

2... 1...

The cannon ball
bounced
off Bart's **chest**
(but didn't leave a **dent**).

The Beastlies **hacked**
with sword and axe,
but each one **broke**
or **bent.**

"To the rigging!" Snapper ordered. "I'll hold him here below." The Beastlies moaned but Snapper raised his hook and shouted, "GO!"

The wind lashed waves to jagged peaks and flicked up foamy flecks.

As Heartless Bart and Snapper faced each other 'cross the deck.

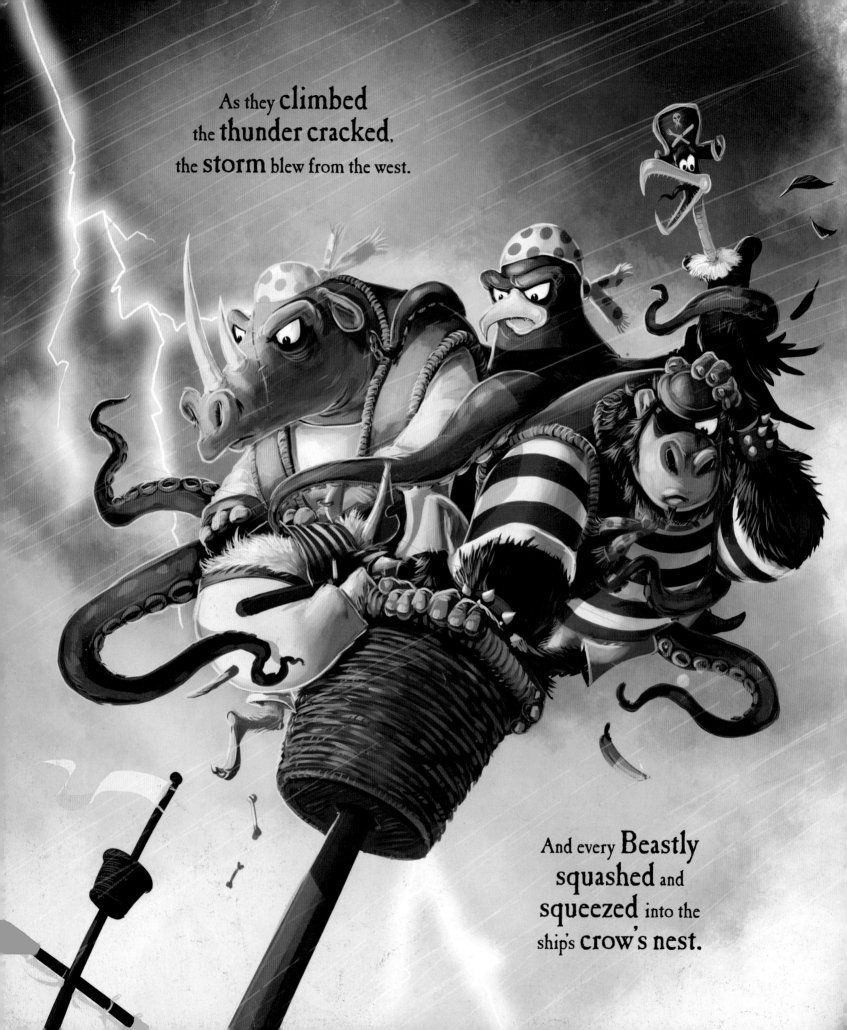

As they **climbed**
the **thunder cracked**,
the **storm** blew from the west.

And every **Beastly**
squashed and
squeezed into the
ship's **crow's nest.**

Bart beat him **back**
towards the mast, then with
one **mighty blow**,

he **cut** the Captain's sword
in **two**, and Snapper **gulped** . . .
"**Uh-oh!**"

He waited for Bart's **final blow**
but it was **never** dealt.
Instead a **hook** from high **above**
dropped **down** and
snagged his belt.

The Beastlies dropped **down** to the deck while Bart shot up the mast! **Up** and up Bart went until the cable **stopped** at last. He **raged** down at the deck below, his face **dark** as the sky.

"Get ready for defeat, you swabs!" and raised his **cutlass** high. But as he leapt down from the mast a single **lightning bolt struck** Bart's sword and **zapped** him with . . .

The cable tightened sharply and **yanked** the metal bully, who was astounded when he found he hung down from a pulley.

He tumbled to the deck below
and landed with a

CRACK!

Right on his shiny metal hat
and everything went black.

Bart woke to find the Beastlies had
cut off his sword and beard,
and made the one and only thing an
armoured pirate feared.

A GIANT metal can-opener!

Bart squealed, jumped up and ran.

"HURRAH!"
The Beastlies cheered.
"Our favourite ...
... Pirate-in-a-Can."

One week **later**,
Tom (The Tankard)
still hadn't heard a peep,
since Heartless Bart sailed
away on Wednesday last week.
Tom knew that with his **armour**
Heartless Bart could **never** fail.
And thought the Beastlies
must be dead
when someone yelled,

"You've mail!"

Amongst the WANTED posters
and the bills for hooks and rum,
was a **postcard** from the Beastlies
— and it was addressed to Tom!

It said,

Thank you for
the VERY tasty
Giant Metal Man!

We ate
the best,
but here's the rest,
saved for you
in a CAN

the
BEASTLIES

TO
TOM. TERROR,
c/o PIRATE
SECRET
HIDEAWAY

To Cathy. All my love.

Thanks to John Mullaney for his metallic help.

Bloomsbury Publishing,
London, Oxford, New York, New Delhi and Sydney

First published in Great Britain in 2016
by Bloomsbury Publishing Plc
50 Bedford Square, London, WC1B 3DP

A CIP catalogue record for this book
is available from the British Library

ISBN 978 1 4088 4986 6 (HB)
ISBN 978 1 4088 4988 0 (PB)
ISBN 978 1 4088 4987 3 (eBook)

Printed in China by Leo Paper Products, Heshan, Guangdong

1 3 5 7 9 10 8 6 4 2

www.bloomsbury.com

BLOOMSBURY is a registered trademark
of Bloomsbury Publishing Plc

All papers used by Bloomsbury Publishing are natural,
recyclable products made from wood
grown in well-managed forests.
The manufacturing processes conform to the
environmental regulations of the country of origin